For all the children who read this

on Christmas night.

M.M.

The truth is that once we weren't children any more we never did believe Grandpa's story, not really, much as we might have wanted to. It was just too improbable, too fantastical. We still loved listening to it, though. Christmas nights would never have been the same without it.

We'd be out there on the hillside, all of us together, keeping watch over the sheep by night. That's where he'd been on the first Christmas night all those years before, the night it happened – or that's what he told us. We'd be wrapped in our cloaks and huddled

round the fire, the sheep
shifting around us in the darkness, and we'd
be ready and waiting for the story to begin.
That's just how it was last night. Grandpa poked
his shepherd's crook into the fire and sent a
shower of sparks flying up into the night sky.

'When I was very little,' he began, 'I remember
I used to think all the stars were made out of
sparks like those, sparks that went on for ever,
that never went out. Then one night, I'd have
been nine, or maybe ten years old, something
quite wonderful happened. Father and Uncle Zac

were there, and my older brothers, Reuben and Jacob. We were all tired and irritable. It had been a long, hard day. We'd lost a couple of lambs the night before, to a wolf maybe, or a jackal. So no one was singing around the fire that night. No one was even talking. I remember I was stabbing at the fire with my crook, making stars of the sparks, as I loved to do. Then it happened.

Instead of flying up high to join the stars, they seemed to be playing with one another, then arranging themselves into a figure, a human figure, that was bathed in sudden glorious light,

hovering over us, wings outstretched. It was
an angel!

I threw myself into Father's arms and buried
my face in his shoulder. When I dared look up
again Uncle Zac and Reuben and Jacob were
lying face down on the ground, Jacob sobbing
like a baby. The sheep had scattered everywhere,
bleating piteously.

"I'm sorry to drop in on you unexpectedly
like this," said the angel. And at the sound of his
voice the sheep fell silent around us. "It must be
an awful shock. But believe me you've got nothing
to worry about, nothing at all."

There was a comforting warmth to his voice, and a gentleness about him that was instantly reassuring. Uncle Zac and Reuben and Jacob were up on their knees by now, their faces filled not with fear, but with awe and wonder. The sheep were drifting back towards us, gazing up at the angel adoringly as if he were their shepherd. It was Uncle Zac who dared to speak first.

"Are you really an angel?" he breathed.

"I am," said the angel. "And my name is Gabriel."

"Are you really real?" Father asked, clutching me as tightly as I was clutching him. "Or are you a dream?"

"No dream," the Angel Gabriel replied. "What I am is real, and what I've come to tell you is true. I bring you news of great joy. For tonight, only a few miles away from here in Bethlehem a child has been born, a Saviour who is Christ the Lord. He will bring peace and goodwill to the whole world. Even as I speak, this child King, this son of God and son of man, is lying wrapped in swaddling clothes and cradled in a manger. I can see from your faces that you don't quite believe me, do you?"

"Kings are born in palaces," said Father.

"Not this King," replied the angel. "But seeing

is believing, isn't it? How would you like to go there? Would you like to see him for yourselves?"

"We'll go, of course we will," said Uncle Zac, getting to his feet. "But you'll have to tell us where to find him. There are dozens of stables in Bethlehem. How are we to know which one he is in?"

"It's simple," the Angel Gabriel said. "When I've gone you'll see a star in the eastern sky. Just follow it and it'll stop right over the stable. That's where you'll find the baby. What are you waiting for? Do you want to go, or don't you?"

"Why us?" asked Uncle Zac. "Why have you chosen us?"

"Because," replied the Angel Gabriel, "because one day he too will be a shepherd as you are, a shepherd not of sheep, but of all mankind."

"I don't like it," Reuben whispered to Uncle Zac. "How do we know it's true? It could be some sort of a trick, to get us to leave our sheep."

"Oh dear," sighed the Angel Gabriel. "I can see you're going to need some convincing."

As he spoke the sky above was suddenly filled with angels, hundreds of them, and the whole earth rang with their singing. "Glory to God on high. And on earth, peace, goodwill towards men."

Even as they sang, they hovered above us,
their wings beating the air so that there was a
great rushing wind all about us that fanned the
embers of the fire into sudden roaring flames.

Reuben and Jacob and Uncle Zac were flat on their faces again, but I watched. I watched all the time. I didn't want to miss a thing. I wasn't frightened at all, I was simply spellbound.

The angels were gone as unexpectedly as they had appeared, the Angel Gabriel too, leaving us alone with our sheep in the silence and the darkness of the hillside. It took a while for our eyes to become accustomed to the dark again. Father threw some more wood onto the fire, and when the sparks flew up I half expected them to become the Angel Gabriel again, but this time they just vanished into the blackness above.

"Look," Uncle Zac whispered. "Look up there in the east. That star! It's moving!"

And sure enough, there it was: a moving star low in the eastern sky, as bright a star as I'd ever seen.

"Come on. Let's follow it," Uncle Zac said. "We have to find out if this saviour has really come. We have to know if the child King is there."

"What about the sheep?" Father asked. "Who'll look after the sheep? We can't just leave them."

"Well, I'm not staying," said Reuben and Jacob in unison.

And suddenly everyone was looking at me and I could see at once the way it was going.

"Why me?" I protested. "What about the wolves? What about the jackals?"

"He's frightened of the dark," Jacob scoffed. "He's a scaredy cat."

"You've got the fire," Uncle Zac told me. "They won't come near the fire."

"We won't be gone long, son." Father might have sounded more sympathetic than my brothers, but he was still going with them. They were still leaving me alone. "Bethlehem's just over the hill. We'll be back before dawn."

"But we could take the sheep with us," I pleaded. "Then we could all go."

"You can't move sheep in the dark, stupid," Reuben said.

"But why me?" I cried. "It's just because I'm the youngest. It's not fair." No one was listening to me.

"Don't worry," said Father, trying to console me as they made ready to go. "We'll tell you all about the baby when we get back. Promise. You just keep the fire going and look after the sheep. You'll be quite safe."

And off they went, shadows drifting away into the night, leaving me. I had never felt so alone, nor so miserable as I did then. Sitting by the fire, pulling my cloak around me, I cursed my luck for being the youngest, and my father for abandoning me, and began to sob my heart out. Lifting my head I let

out a huge wail of anger and despair
that echoed over the hills.

"It's not fair! It's not fair!"

As the echoes died I became
suddenly aware that I was not alone
any more. There, opposite me in
the glowing light of the fire,
sat the Angel Gabriel.

"You don't sound very happy," he said.
"They left you behind, didn't they? Well someone
had to look after the sheep, I suppose."
"I suppose," I said, so relieved not to
be alone any more.

"You're right though," said the Angel Gabriel, "about life not being fair. So I've had this idea, to make it a little fairer. I could fly you there to the stable. We could be there and back, lickety-split, and no one would ever know you'd been gone."

"You could fly me there?" I cried, more excited than I had been in all my life. "You could really do that?"

"Easy as pie," he said.

At that moment a sheep
and her lamb came and lay down
beside me, as if to remind me of my duty.
I knew I couldn't leave them.

"The sheep," I said, suddenly downcast.
"There'd be no one to look after the sheep."

"Have you forgotten my heavenly chorus?" said the
Angel Gabriel. "They don't just sing, you know."

And even as he spoke the sky above us burst into
light and out of the light they came floating down –
who knows how many? – landing softly on their feet
in amongst the sheep who seemed not in the least
alarmed.

"Enough to do the job,

I think, don't you?" laughed the

Angel Gabriel. "Now, hop on. We haven't

a moment to lose."

I did as he told me. Still clutching my shepherd's

crook, I vaulted onto his back and clung on.

So I left the sheep with their guardian angels and

lifted off, my arms around the Angel Gabriel's neck.

"Hang on," he said laughing, "but don't throttle

me, there's a good lad."

And so we rose into the sky, leaving the

sheep below with the guardian angels now as

their shepherds.

On we flew along black glassy rivers,
up and down hills, his great wings beating strongly,
slowly. And always we went eastwards,
the star ahead of us, beckoning us on. I wanted it to
go on for ever and ever, even though the cold numbed
my fingers, numbed my face, and made my eyes water.
I saw the lights of the little town flickering beneath
us. We saw where the star had stopped, saw the lights
of the stable below. We floated gently to earth in
the courtyard of an inn.

The town lay asleep all around us, still and
silent, except for a couple of dogs that barked at
one another.

Cats slunk everywhere into dark alleyways, their eyes glinting.

"You go in alone," said the Angel Gabriel. "His mother is called Mary, his father is Joseph. Off you go now."

The guttering glow of yellow lamplight seemed to be inviting me in. The door was half open. I stepped in.

It was much like any other stable I'd been in – warm and dusty and smelly. A couple of donkeys were lying side by side, their great ears following me, their eyes watching me with dreamy indifference.

In the dim light of the stable I could see several oxen chewing their cud, grunting contentedly. One of them licked deep into her nose as I passed by. I could still see no baby, no Christ child, no King. I was beginning to wonder if the angel had brought me to the wrong place. Then from a stall at the far end of the stable came a man's voice.

"We're over here," he said. "Where the sheep are. Careful you don't tread on them."

The sheep shifted as I walked slowly through them. A lamb came skittering out of the shadows and suckled his mother furiously, his tail waggling with wild delight.

It was then I saw them, at last, their faces bright in the lamplight.

"Come closer," said Mary. "You won't be disturbing him. He's wide awake."

She was sitting propped up in the hay, the baby cradled in her arms. All I could see of him was a pink face and one tiny hand which he waved a little and then promptly shoved in his mouth. He was looking at me, straight at me, and when at last he took his fist out of his mouth, he smiled, and it was a smile I have never forgotten, a smile of such love that it moves my heart to this day whenever I think of it.

I crouched down in the straw beside them and when I offered him my finger, he clung onto it and didn't seem to want to let go.

"He's strong," I said.

"He'll need to be," said Joseph.

We talked in whispers, the three of us, and Joseph told me how ashamed he was not to have found a better place for Mary to give birth, but that everywhere in Bethlehem, all the inns, were full.

"It's fine," said Mary. "It's warm in here and his manger's full of soft hay for a cradle. He has all he needs, and now he has his first visitor. Would you like to hold him for a while?"

I had never in all my life held a baby before –
plenty of lambs, but never a baby. Joseph showed
me how to do it. Babies were easier, I discovered.
They didn't wriggle so much.

"What's he called?" I asked, cradling him in my arms, hoping against hope he wouldn't cry.

"Jesus," Mary said. "We're calling him Jesus."

So for a few precious minutes I held him in my arms, the child that has been the light of my life ever since.

I stayed until they laid him in his manger of hay, until he fell asleep, and Mary too. Then Joseph took me back through the sheep to the stable door to say goodbye.

"There may be more visitors tonight," said Joseph. "But you were the first. We shan't forget you."

"Nor I you," I replied. It was only then, as I was about to go, that it occurred to me I had forgotten something.

"Whenever a child is born in our village," I said, "everyone brings a present. This is all I've got with me." And I handed Joseph my shepherd's crook. "Father made it for me. He said it should last a lifetime."

"Thank you," Joseph said, running his hand along the crook. "This is wonderful work, the work of a craftsman. He will have no finer gift than this." And with that he turned and went back inside.

Moments later the Angel Gabriel was winging

me away, out over the walls of the stable
yard, over the sleeping town, away
from the light of the star and
back towards the darkness
of the hills.

As we flew I was full
of questions. I wanted to
know so much about Jesus,
this child King who was
going to save the world.

"How will he do it?" I shouted
into Gabriel's ear against the sound of
the wind. "How will he bring us peace and goodwill?"

The Angel Gabriel flew on, never answering any
of my questions. It was almost as if he hadn't heard
me at all. Only when we landed in amongst the
sheep and the shepherd angels did he at last give
me an answer.

"Love," he said. "He will bring us love, and through love we will at last have peace and goodwill on earth. Now, make sure you keep the fire going, there's a good lad."

Those were the last words he spoke to me.
There were no goodbyes. There was no time.
He rose at once into the night sky, and with him all
the other angels too, each a beacon of sparkling light.
And as they went I heard first the singing of their
wings, then the singing of their voices until the
sky above me and the whole earth rang with such
a joyful sound that I thought my heart would burst.

"Glory to God on high. And on earth, peace,
goodwill towards men."

Slowly the music faded and the light died.

I felt suddenly alone in the night until the sheep gathered about me, all of us, I know, sharing the wonder of everything we had just witnessed.

Father and the others came back just after sunrise, full of everything, of course, and very pleased with themselves. They'd followed the star and found the stable and the child King wrapped in swaddling clothes. He'd been fast asleep in his manger, they said, all the time they were there.

"Such a pity you couldn't have been with us," Reuben sniggered.

"Then these three Kings from far off Persian lands turned up, and there wasn't room for us and we had to go," said Uncle Zac, who sounded more than a little put out. "You should've seen the presents they brought: gold, frankincense, myrrh.

We had nothing to give him except our crooks and we couldn't hardly give him those, could we?"

"Proper stupid we felt," Jacob added.

"Sheep all right?" Father asked me. "Anything happen while we were gone?"

"Not a thing," I replied. "Not a thing."

I nearly told them then, so nearly. I was bursting to tell them everything. But I didn't, because I knew they'd never have believed me anyway. Reuben and Jacob would only have scoffed and laughed at me even more than usual.

Just keep quiet about it, I told myself.

When the time comes you can tell your children and your grandchildren, because they'll know about Jesus by then – everyone will.

And you do too, don't you, his whole life, everything he did and said. You may not believe my story but you don't laugh at me, you don't scoff. You just think I'm a bit old, a bit doolally. And I suppose I am at that.'

And Grandpa always ended his story the same way, his voice almost a whisper. 'And that shepherd's crook I gave him – I told Father I'd lost it in the dark that night and he made me another – Jesus carried it with him all his life. It was there at the Sermon

on the Mount; when he fed the
five thousand; when he rode into
Jerusalem. He had it with him almost
to the end, till they took it off him,
till that last day when he carried the cross instead.'

*And so Grandpa finished his story. But that wasn't
the end of it, not last night. Last night the story had
a very different ending altogether, something amazing,
incredible – which is why I've written it down at once.
This way I'll always be able to remember it as it was
and I'll never be able to believe it didn't happen.
As we sat there around the fire, silent in our thoughts,
I thought, as all of us did, that Grandpa's Christmas*

story was over for another year. It was such a lovely story, but just a story. We knew how Grandpa had followed Jesus all his life, how much he loved him. Wishful thinking, we thought, that's all it had been, just wishful thinking. But I remember sitting there last night and wondering whether any of it could possibly be true. That was when it happened.

Grandpa began prodding at the fire with his shepherd's crook. Showers of sparks rose into the night

sky and as I watched them I saw that they did
not fly up towards the stars, but gathered themselves
into a great light. And within the light I saw beacons
of brightness that took shape and became angels,
hundreds of them, thousands of them, their wings singing
in the air, then their voices too, until the skies above us
rang with such joyful sounds that I thought my heart
would burst.

'Glory to God on high!' they sang. 'And on earth,
peace, goodwill towards men!'